Stella Batts

A Case of the Meanies

Stella Batts

A Case of the Meanies

BOOK

Courtney Sheinmel

Illustrated by Jennifer A. Bell

For Avery Elana and Chase Benjamin
Happy 6th birthday
—Courtney

For Elaina
—Jennifer

Text Copyright © 2012 Courtney Sheinmel
Illustrations Copyright © 2012 Jennifer A. Bell

Sleeping Bear Press™

315 East Eisenhower Parkway, Suite 200 • Ann Arbor, MI 48108 • www.sleepingbearpress.com
© Sleeping Bear Press, a part of Cengage Learning.

Hot Tamales® is a trademark of Just Born, Inc., Bethlehem, PA, USA. Pop Rocks® is a registered trademark of Zeta Espacial S.A. Tootsie Roll® is a registered trademarks of Tootsie Roll Industries, LLC.

Printed and bound in the United States.
10 9 8 7 6 5 4 3 2 1

Library of Congress Cataloging-in-Publication Data • Sheinmel, Courtney • Stella Batts : a case of the meanies / Courtney Sheinmel. • p. cm. • Summary: "Everyone is invited to a birthday party at her parent's candy store, except Stella Batts. She needs to figure out to be a pleasant hostess when she's not on the guest list" • ISBN 978-1-58536-199-1 (pbk.) • ISBN 978-1-58536-198-4 (hard cover) • [1. Interpersonal relations–Fiction. 2. Parties–Fiction. 3. Family life–California–Fiction. 4. California–Fiction.] • I. Title. II. Title: Case of the meanies. • PZ7.S54124Ssm 2012 • [Fic]–dc23 • 2012022775

Table of Contents

Prologue
(Another Word
for Introduction)

Hey, it's me, Stella Batts! I'm back again!

In case you haven't read my other books or you just don't remember them so well, I'll tell you a few things about me:

1. I live in Somers, California, with my parents and my sister, Penny.

2. Soon I'll live with my brother Jack, too. But not yet, because Mom's still pregnant with him.

3. We own a candy store called Batts

Confections.

4. Okay, so I guess my parents are the owners, not Penny and me. But there are things named for us in the store—like Stella's Fudge, and the Penny Candy Wall.

5. When the baby gets born, something will be named for him too, but not until then because Mom says that's bad luck.

6. Also she and Dad keep changing their minds about his name, though Mom says Jack is the absolute final choice. Anyway, that's not really about me, and this is my list.

7. I'm eight years old, which means I'm in third grade.

8. Writing is one of my favorite things to do. Obviously.

CHAPTER 1

Story Ingredients

This morning our teacher, Mrs. Finkel, told us that part of our homework will be to write a story. Some kids groaned because they didn't want to do it, but I was super excited.

(But just so you know, what you're reading right now is NOT my homework, because this is going to be longer than a story—this is going to be a full book. My FOURTH book, as a matter of fact.)

Mrs. Finkel said we should work on our

stories every night this week: tonight, which is Monday, and also Tuesday, Wednesday, and Thursday. But not Friday, because that's when we're supposed to hand them in to her. Anyway, she's not allowed to give us homework on Friday nights. I bet Mrs. Finkel wishes she could. She's really strict. But the rule in our school is you don't get weekend homework until fifth grade—that's two more years away.

"What should our stories be about?" Clark asked.

"Anything you want," Mrs. Finkel said. "Now pull out a piece of paper. I want you all to write down your characters, your setting, and your plot—those are the three ingredients to every story. Characters are who the story is about, the setting is where it takes place, and the plot is what happens."

I already knew all of that, because I've written three books, and books are just really long stories.

I didn't even have to think that hard. Here's what I wrote:

Stella's Story

1. Characters—me and the people I know
2. Setting—Somers, CA, because that's where we live
3. Plot—some things that happen to us, but you'll just have to read to the end of the book to find out all of that

There. All done.

I looked down the row. Next to me, Spencer was chewing on the end of his pencil. He does that when he's thinking.

Lucy raised her hand. I watched her rest

her elbow on her desk, and then switch arms when the first one got tired. "Excuse me, Mrs. Finkel?" she said finally.

"Yes, Lucy?" Mrs. Finkel said.

"Our characters don't have to be people, do they?"

"Duh, of course they do," Joshua piped up from the back row.

"No calling out, Joshua," Mrs. Finkel said. "You know that's Disruptive Behavior."

"But Lucy called out," he said.

"Lucy was trying to get my attention, and she did so very politely. 'Duh' is not a polite word to use with your classmates."

I don't think Joshua cares about being polite. He uses the word "duh" a lot. I mean A LOT.

"To answer your question, Lucy," Mrs. Finkel continued, "no they don't have to be people. Your character can be a polar bear, or a flamingo. Or a fictional person—that means made up." I already knew that word. "Or your character doesn't have to be alive. It can be a statue, or a piggy bank or a potted plant."

"Potted plants are alive," Joshua piped up without raising his hand and waiting to be called on. Mrs. Finkel turned to glare at him. He clapped his hand over his mouth so no more words would come out.

"Yes," Mrs. Finkel said. You could tell she didn't really like being corrected—especially by Joshua. "Plants are technically alive, but I meant your characters can be anything you want."

"Cool, thanks," Lucy said.

Around the room there were sounds of people erasing things, blowing on the little bits of eraser to get them off the page, and then scribbling more stuff down. I folded my hands on my desk. That's what you're supposed to do when you're done with your work.

"Oooh, oooh, oooh!!" someone called out. I didn't even have to turn around to know it was Joshua. That's the sound he makes when he wants Mrs. Finkel to call on him, even though you're just supposed to raise your hand *quietly*. Also he waves his arm around in the air, like he's signaling an airplane.

"Joshua, you're disrupting the other students," Mrs. Finkel said.

"But I have to tell you something."

"Then you can raise your hand quietly."

"You were looking down at your desk,"

Joshua said. "If I raised my hand quietly, you wouldn't have seen me. That's why you let Lucy call out before, remember?"

"I'm looking at you now," Mrs. Finkel said. "Let's try this again."

Joshua raised his hand quietly.

"Yes, Joshua?"

"I wanted my character to be a dragon, but I just saw that Asher wrote dragon on his paper."

"Your eyes shouldn't be on anyone's paper but your own," Mrs. Finkel said. "Asher can write about whatever he wants to write about, and you can write about whatever you want to write about."

Joshua slammed his hand down on his desk. "But then there will be TWO stories about dragons, and I wanted mine to be the only one!"

"I think you need to take a trip to Mr. O'Neil's office to calm down," Mrs. Finkel told Joshua. Mr. O'Neil is our principal.

"You can't send me to Mr. O'Neil! It's my birthday!"

"Today is your birthday?" Mrs. Finkel asked.

"On Friday it will be," Joshua said.

That means this is just his birth WEEK. You can totally get punished on your birth week.

"Well, disruptive behavior is not allowed, no matter what day it is," Mrs. Finkel told him. She wrote a note for Joshua to take to Mr. O'Neil and Joshua stomped out of the room. That counted as even more disruptive behavior.

After that, Mrs. Finkel said we should be done and she asked for a volunteer to collect

the papers. A bunch of kids raised their hands.
Nobody said "Oooh, oooh, oooh," because
they didn't want to get into trouble.

I raised my hand too, but Mrs. Finkel
called on Evie. I think it's because Evie just
moved here from England, so she's still Mrs.
Finkel's favorite.

Evie came by my desk and I handed my

list to her. She passed the pile to Mrs. Finkel. "I'll get these back to you by the end of the day," Mrs. Finkel said.

Joshua shoved open the door to the classroom just as we were about to start our math lesson. "Smella!" he yelled, which is his nickname for me, ever since I fell down on our class nature walk and landed right smack in the middle of something so disgusting I don't even want to write about it. Besides, I already said what it was in my first book.

Whenever he calls me that, I know all the kids are remembering what happened. I hate that. Mom says Joshua will forget about calling me Smella eventually. So far he hasn't. Maybe he has such a good memory that he'll remember to call me Smella for the rest of his life.

A few kids snickered this time. I felt

my cheeks get super hot—the way they get whenever I eat Hot Tamales candies at Batts Confections. I bet my cheeks were turning just as red as Hot Tamales, too.

"Joshua!" Mrs. Finkel said in her sternest voice. I wondered if he would be sent back to Mr. O'Neil's office for being disruptive AGAIN. No one in our class has ever been sent to the principal twice in one day.

"Sorry," Joshua said. "I meant *Stella*. I have something to tell her."

"I'm sure it can wait until after school," Mrs. Finkel told him. "Take your seat."

She went on to teach us our math lesson. Afterward we had to do two pages in our math notebooks. That's when Mrs. Finkel started looking over everyone's story notes. I could tell that's what she was doing because I'm in the front row. When I looked up, I saw her flipping through them.

She caught me looking at her and I looked down quickly, blushing again—though I could tell it wasn't as bad as the last time. My cheeks felt a little warmer than usual, so maybe they were just pink, like a stick of bubblegum.

"Stella, can you come here a minute?" Mrs. Finkel asked.

I went up to her desk. This girl Maddie's story was at the top of the pile of story lists. Mrs. Finkel had written ✔ on the top. Checks are what we get on most of our assignments. It means, "This is good work."

Mrs. Finkel thumbed through the pile and pulled out my paper. She tapped it with her pencil. It didn't have a check mark on it.

"Are you sure you understood the assignment?" she asked.

"Yes," I said.

"It's all right if you didn't," Mrs. Finkel said. "I know this is third grade and you're just learning about how to write a story."

"Actually I've written lots of books," I told her. Okay, only three. But that's a lot for an eight-year-old!

"You didn't give much of a plot description."

"That's because you don't get to know the end of a story until you read it." *Duh*, I wanted to tell her, like Joshua would. But I'd never say that to a teacher. I'd never say that to anyone.

Okay, maybe I'd say it to Penny. But she's my little sister, and things you say to your little sister are different than things you'd say to anyone else.

"That's part of story writing," Mrs. Finkel said. "The author gets to know what happens at the end before the readers do. It's okay to put those details here, though."

"But not everything has happened yet."

"I see," Mrs. Finkel said. *I see* is another way grownups say *I understand*. But the way Mrs. Finkel was looking at me, kind of frowning so she got a little wrinkle between her eyes, I could tell she didn't really understand at all.

She picked up the whole pile of kids' papers and shuffled them together so the edges matched up. "Why don't you do the honor of handing these back to your classmates?"

I shrugged my shoulders. "Okay," I said.

"Think about the plot a bit at home tonight. Maybe you'll be inspired. Do you know what that word means?"

Of course I did! It's when something gives you the feeling to want to do something. Things inspire me to write my books all the time. "Yes, I know," I told Mrs. Finkel.

"We can discuss it again tomorrow, if you want," she said.

I knew I would NOT want to do that. Mrs. Finkel handed me the pile and I went around the room, giving each paper back to the right person. Every single kid had a check mark on top of his or her page. Some kids even had a check plus, which is what Mrs. Finkel writes when she thinks our work is better than good.

Joshua's list was the last in the pile. Even he had a check mark. I handed it over to him.

"I saw Penny in the principal's office," he said. "That's what I wanted to tell you."

CHAPTER 2

After School

As soon as the bell rang at the end of the day, I ran outside to find Penny. The kindergarteners get out of school five minutes before everyone else, so I knew she'd be waiting for me. I always meet Penny, her friend Zoey, and whoever is picking us up that day right by the flagpole next to the parking lot.

Evie raced to catch up with me—she's part of our carpool too, but she couldn't run as fast because she was in silver sparkly shoes instead of sneakers. For clothes she had on a pink plaid skirt and a white blouse. It wasn't school picture day or anything. That's how Evie always dresses. I don't think she even owns any clothes that aren't fancy.

When we got to the usual meeting spot, Penny wasn't there.

"Penny's in trouble!" Zoey called out.

Then she filled Evie and me in on what happened.

There's a new boy in Penny's kindergarten class. At lunchtime, he asked Penny to trade her candy for his celery. She didn't want to. Obviously. Who would want celery instead of candy? Not me! But the new boy got mad and called Penny a baby. That's when Penny stomped on his foot. REALLY hard. Then Miss Griffin sent Penny to Mr. O'Neil's office.

Miss Griffin is Penny's kindergarten

teacher. I had her too, but she never sent me to the principal's office. In fact, NO ONE has ever sent me to the principal. I don't even know what his office looks like!

"Where is Penny now?" I asked Zoey. "Still with Mr. O'Neil?"

"No. But he called her parents."

"They're also my parents," I reminded her.

"Right. And her dad—"

"He's also my dad."

"Yeah, yeah, I know. He came to pick her up as soon as school was over. He said she couldn't come over because she's not allowed to have a play date after she stomps on someone's foot. Penny said it wasn't fair."

That's exactly what Penny would say about something like that. *It's not fair* is the sentence she says the most out of all the sentences in the world.

"Really it's not fair to *me*," Zoey continued. "Because I didn't stomp on anyone's foot and now I don't get a play date. It's all Bruce's fault!"

"Now, now, Zoey," Mrs. Benson said. Mrs. Benson is Zoey's mom, and also the Monday carpool driver. My best friend Willa's dad used to drive carpool on Mondays. But Willa's family moved to Pennsylvania and the whole schedule got switched around.

"But it's true!" Zoey insisted. "It's not fair!"

We pulled up outside Evie's house a few minutes later.

Actually, Evie doesn't live in a house. She lives in an apartment. Except she doesn't say apartment. She says flat. Here are some more things she says:

1. Chips instead of French fries

2. Lift instead of elevator

3. Loo instead of bathroom

It's because she's from England. She has a really cool accent, too. But get this— she thinks I'm the one with an accent! An American accent!

Anyway, back to the story.

Evie's dad was waiting for us on the sidewalk. He works at home instead of in an office. He's an artist. Sometimes he paints things and sometimes he draws things on the computer that go up on websites.

"Hi Dad," Evie said.

"Hi girls," Mr. King said. "How's your mom feeling?" he asked me. People always ask how she's feeling since she's been pregnant.

"She's fine," I said.

"Where's Bella?" Evie asked. Bella is her puppy. She's a Maltese, which is a kind of dog that looks like a ball of marshmallow fluff.

"She's taking a little nap back at the apartment. I think I tired her out during our walk."

"I can't wait to show you Bella's new trick," Evie told me. "I taught her to sit—in English and French. I want her to be bilingual, like I am."

Evie is the only third grader in our school taking French. She started it at her old school. Now she gets private lessons with Mrs. Blank in the learning lab. The rest of us will start language classes in fourth grade, but Evie's been teaching me some words so I'll be ahead like she is.

Most words I still don't know. "How do you say 'sit'?" I asked her.

She said something that sounded like "Ah-see," but since it was another language, I knew the spelling was probably different. "How do you spell it?" I asked.

"A-S-S-I-S," she said.

I'd have to add that to the list I have at home–Stella's French Words.

"It must be hard to teach a dog to sit in TWO languages," I said.

"Not at all," Evie said. "When I see her

sitting, I say 'sit' and 'assis.' Then I give her a treat, so she knows she's done something right."

Evie, her dad, and I walked up the path to apartment number 307—that's where the Kings live. "Is Mum home?" Evie asked.

Mr. King shook his head. "She had a trip today, remember?" Evie's mom is a flight attendant. When she has trips, Mr. King takes care of Evie.

He unlocked the door and pushed it open. "Bella!" Evie called.

"Shh, honey, I told you she was sleeping," Mr. King said.

"But she always comes to greet me when I get home from school," Evie said. "She smells me coming up the walkway because she has a particularly keen sense of smell."

Evie sometimes talks like a grownup. I think that happens when you're from England, but I'm not sure because Evie's the only kid I know who comes from there.

"Also because she knows how much I miss her," Evie continued.

"Did you miss your old dad that much?" Mr. King asked.

"Not quite as much," Evie admitted. "Sorry Dad."

Here's something funny: Evie says "Dad"

just like American kids do, but she calls her mom "Mum."

"Oh, bother," Mr. King said.

"What?" Evie asked.

"I just realized I forgot to fetch the mail. I'm expecting a work call in the next few minutes. Would you girls mind getting it?"

We both shook our heads no.

"Just don't run out in the street."

"Duh," Evie said.

"That's how you talk now that you're in America?"

"No, not really," Evie said. "That's just what a boy in school always says."

Inside, we could hear the phone start to ring. Mr. King handed Evie his mailbox key. The two of us headed back out.

In Hilltop Acres, all the mailboxes for all the different apartments are in the same

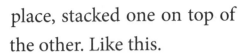

place, stacked one on top of the other. Like this.

It's a smart idea to have a key to open the mailbox, so no one can steal anything. At my house, our mailbox is at the end of the driveway, and it doesn't have a key. Not that anyone has ever stolen our mail, but you never know.

Evie inserted the key into the lock and opened the mailbox. She pulled out a bunch of envelopes and a magazine, and she handed it all over for me to hold while she locked the mailbox back up. I sorted things into size order: the magazine was biggest, then two white envelopes that looked like bills, and then a tiny blue envelope.

Wait a second! The front of the blue envelope said: Miss Evie King. "You got something," I told her.

"My first mail in Somers!"

"Did you get a lot of mail in England?" I asked.

"No, just for my birthday and such things. I haven't had a birthday since we've been here."

"Is it your birthday soon?" That's the only time I get mail, too.

"Not for months."

I handed it over. "Open it now," I said.

She did. Inside was a blue card with red letters:

JOSHUA LEWIS IS TURNING NINE!
Join the celebration at Batts Confections
Friday, 4–6 p.m.

Joshua Lewis is the same Joshua who's in our class. I told Evie in case she didn't know

JOSHUA LEWIS
IS TURNING
NINE!
JOIN THE CELEBRATION
AT BATTS CONFECTIONS
FRIDAY, 4-6 P.M.

his last name.

We walked up the sidewalk, back to her house. "You didn't tell me he was having a party at your store," she said.

"I didn't know," I told her. How come Mom and Dad didn't tell me? New rule: From now on, if anyone from my class wanted to have a party at the store, they had to tell me first.

"That's probably why he invited me," she said.

"What do you mean?" I asked.

"I bet you'll have the invitation waiting for you at home. He had to invite you, because it's your store. Then he probably invited me because I'm your best friend."

Evie is really my second-best friend.

Willa is my first-best friend—but she moved to Pennsylvania last month, so Evie is my best friend who lives in Somers.

"But I don't think he should get to have a party in your store since he's a meanie," Evie continued. "He made Asher feel bad about his dragon story."

"I'd rather read Asher's story than Joshua's," I said.

"Me too," Evie agreed.

We got back to number 307. When Evie pulled open the door, a little ball of marshmallow fluff fur popped out.

"Bella!" I said. "You woke up!"

"You see, she does smell me coming up the walkway," Evie said. She reached down. But just as she was about to scoop Bella up, she ran off, a marshmallow streak down the steps, across the garden and straight out to the main sidewalk.

Mr. King had told us to avoid the street. Now Bella was headed right toward it. What if she ran into the street and got hit by a car?

"Bella!" we both called after her. "Bella, stop!"

CHAPTER 3

Stella Superhero

We started to chase after her. She's just a little pup, with eensy weensy little legs, like stumpy Tootsie Rolls, but she was running like she had long legs, like lollypop sticks, carrying her down the sidewalk, past the mailboxes.

"Stop! Stop!" Evie called out.

"Stop! Stop!" I echoed her.

Two more steps, and Bella would be in the street. A red car turned at the corner. Oh no, oh no, OH NO!!! "Bella!" I shouted. "Sit!

Assis!!!"

In my head I thought, *Please listen to me, Bella. Please!* I wanted to click my heels like Dorothy in *The Wizard of Oz* and make a wish but there was no time.

But then something amazing happened. Bella stopped right where she was. Evie reached her and scooped her up. She handed the mail and keys over to me, because her arms were full of puppy fluff. The red car zoomed past. "Oh, Bells, it's okay. You're safe and sound," Evie said in her most reassuring voice. She lifted her hand to wipe a tear off her cheek.

Bella didn't look like she'd ever been worried that she wouldn't be safe and sound.

"Thank you, Stella," Evie said. "You saved her life!"

When we got back to the apartment,

Evie gave Bella a treat so she'd know she did something right by sitting down at the curb, even though I thought Bella had probably forgotten all about it by then.

"Girls," Mr. King called. "You took quite a long time. I was just about to go looking for you."

"Bella got out," Evie said, and she filled him in on all the rest of it.

"Stella is quite handy to have around," Mr. King said. "She rescued my keys from the truck when we first moved here, and she rescued the dog today. I can see it on the cover of a book—*Stella Batts, Superhero!*"

"We're writing books at school," Evie told him. "Well, stories."

"Brilliant," Mr. King said. "Tell me about them."

"Mine's about my best friends' birthday party—my two best friends, Sara and Tesa," Evie said. "They're twins, so they always have a party together. This year it was a going-away party for me too, at Buckingham Palace—that's where the queen lives."

Oh my goodness, the palace where the queen lives! An actual, real-life palace!

I've never been in a palace. At Batts Confections, we have one room made up to look like the dining room in a castle. I think palaces and castles are the same thing. But even so, all we have is one fake room.

"Did you go to the palace a lot when you were in England? Did you ever see the Crown Jewels?"

We have candy Crown Jewels at our store—cookies in the shapes of crowns, with rock candies stuck on, meant to look like emeralds and rubies. They're really cool, but I bet the real Crown Jewels are even better.

"I've never actually been inside the palace," Evie said.

"But what about the party?"

"It was at a pizza place called Da Mario's, unfortunately."

"You love Da Mario's,"

Mr. King said.

"Yeah, but it's kind of ordinary for a story. I wanted things to be a bit more posh so I switched it up."

"So you changed the setting, but not the plot or the characters," I said. *See, Mrs. Finkel, I thought to myself. I know about story writing!*

"Precisely," Evie said. "But I had to add a couple more characters, like Queen Elizabeth and her lady-in-waiting, naturally."

"Naturally," I said. "I bet it was a much better party than Joshua's party will be."

"What party?" Mr. King asked.

"This boy in our class named Joshua is having a party at Stella's candy shop."

"That sounds like fun," Mr. King said.

"Except he's the class meanie," I told him.

"He's done loads of mean things," Evie added. "He calls her Smella." She nodded toward me. I wish she hadn't said that. Even though I'm pretty sure Mr. King knows I'm a clean, non-smelly girl. "And he calls out in class. When he gets caught, he puts his hand over his mouth, like this." Evie smacked her hand on her mouth, just like Joshua.

"Like he just started talking by accident," I said, "even though you know it was on purpose."

"Yup," Evie agreed, dropping her hand back down. "I think he should keep his hand over his mouth all day long. He can take it off just when he needs to eat."

"Or when he's sleeping," I said. "Because then he won't be talking."

"Maybe he will be," Evie said. "I've talked in my sleep before, right Dad?"

"That's right. Sometimes Mum and I go in to check on you and we can tell what you're

dreaming."

"But we're not there when Joshua is sleeping so we wouldn't have to listen to him," I said.

"He'll definitely be talking at his own birthday party, though," Evie said. "Saying all his mean meanie things. It won't be fun at all."

"It sounds to me like you girls are being the meanies, just now," Mr. King said.

When he said that, my cheeks warmed up a little bit. I knew I was blushing—not the Hot-Tamales kind of blushing, but the pink-stick-of-bubblegum kind.

"But Dad, you don't understand," Evie started.

"I understand," Mr. King said. "You're saying this boy Joshua isn't so pleasant to be around. But maybe he acts mean because he's lonely."

"If he's lonely, he should be nicer," Evie said.

"Sometimes it's hard to be nice when you're feeling bad," Mr. King said. "Like when we first moved to Somers and you hadn't met Stella yet. You were feeling lonely and that made you a bit cross with Mum and me.

Remember that?"

Evie nodded. "I remember."

I remembered it, too. She didn't even want to be my friend.

"But Joshua didn't just move here," Evie said.

"There are all sorts of things to be lonely about," Mr. King told her.

"I suppose I should go to this party, then," Evie said.

"I suppose you should, sweets," Mr. King said.

"I should probably go too," I said. "It is my store, and if I don't go, it would be two wrongs not making a right—that's what my friend Willa always says."

"Right on, girls," Mr. King said. "Kill them with kindness, I always say."

Actually he didn't say "Kill THEM with

kindness." He said "Kill 'EM with kindness." He left off the "TH" sound, but I knew what he meant.

"You don't always say that," Evie said. "And besides, we don't want to kill anyone."

"It's an expression. It means you should be extra kind, and maybe you'll knock the mean part right out of him."

"Maybe," Evie said. Though I wasn't sure about that.

The phone rang right then. This time it was my dad, calling to say he was on his way to pick me up.

CHAPTER 4

The Idea

"It's not fair!"

Those were the first words I heard when Dad and I walked in the door. Can you guess who said them? If you said Penny, then you'd be right. I couldn't see her, but I could hear her.

Dad had a bag from Batts Confections. It was silver, with BATTS CONFECTIONS in red letters. He put it down on the shelf in the front hall. That's the same shelf where Mom puts the mail. I flipped through the pile, but there was only grownup stuff. That means bills, bills, bills.

Dad and I were taking our shoes off, as we always do before we walk around the house, when Mom came out from the kitchen to say hello. "Where's Pen?" Dad asked.

"In her room, moping," Mom said. "I think she's a bit embarrassed."

"Have you been able to get the story out of her?" Dad asked.

"Something about the baby," Mom said. "I was just about to go check on her again."

"Wait, where's the rest of the mail?" I asked.

"That's it, on the shelf."

"But I didn't see Joshua's birthday invitation. And how come you didn't tell me he was having his party at the store, anyway?"

"I didn't schedule anything at the store for Joshua," Dad said.

"Oh, I did," Mom said. "Sorry, hon. I've been pretty distracted with this baby stuff."

"Are you sure the invitation didn't come? Evie got hers, and maybe you were distracted about the mail, too."

Mom shook her head. "That's just the way of the post office. You can mail a stack of invitations, but if they're all headed out to different places, sometimes they don't get there at the exact same time. The party's on Friday, right?"

I nodded. "Evie and I don't like him, but we decided we'll go anyway."

Speaking of things I don't like: "Something smells fishy," I added.

"I'm marinating the salmon," Mom said. "It will be ready in an hour, along with asparagus and rice."

Here's my plan for when I grow up. I'll make dinners that are always delicious. Mondays will be spaghetti-and-meatball night, and my kids will be allowed to use as much shaky cheese as they want. The more cheese the better. In fact, everyone'll have their own personal bottle of cheese. Tuesdays we'll have hot dogs and French fries. Wednesdays can be shrimp, which is the only kind of seafood that I like to eat. And Thursdays . . . okay, I haven't decided on the Thursday meal yet, or any of the rest of the days of the week.

Monday   Tuesday   Wednesd

But I'll write them down as soon as I figure it out.

"I don't really like salmon or asparagus," I told Mom.

"I'm sorry to hear that," she said. "That's all we've got."

"But if you eat it, there's a treat from the store in your future," Dad added. "Stuart's brainchild."

"Stuart's what?"

"Brainchild," Dad said. "It's another word for invention."

"Oh, I get it," I said. "What kind of kid would your brain have? The invention kind!"

"Exactly," Dad said.

"That's a cool word," I said. "What is his brainchild this time?"

"If I tell you, it would ruin the surprise."

"I don't need a surprise," I said.

"Oh really, so I should just give Penny *both* treats to eat?"

"No!" I said. "I just mean if you tell me now, I'll get to think about what the treat is and be excited for longer. But if you don't tell me, maybe I'll think it's something I'm not in the mood for and I won't even eat my salmon."

"That's a good argument, Stella," Dad said. "Perhaps you'll be a lawyer when you grow up."

"No, I'm going to be a writer," I reminded him. "Actually I have to write a story for school. But I don't think Mrs. Finkel—"

"I said it's not fair!" Penny shouted again from her room, interrupting me.

"Oh dear," Mom said. "I'm going to try talking to her again."

"I'll go," Dad told her. "Stel, want to come with me? Maybe you can help cheer up your sister."

"I am NOT a baby," Penny told us when we walked into her room. "*Bruce* is."

"I can't believe you really stomped on his foot," I said.

"I don't want to talk about him!" Penny yelled.

"I'm not the one who brought him up," I said.

"Hey, darling," Dad said. I knew he was talking to me and not Penny, since I'm the one he calls darling. "Why don't you finish up your homework, and let me chat with Penny?"

That's the kind of question called rhetorical. You say it like this: reh-tor-i-cul. It means you don't really have to answer the question, just do what I say.

It was his idea for me to even be in Penny's room, but I left the two of them alone, picked up my backpack from the front hall, and sat down at my desk.

I had two different things to do for homework—the story list and the second half of a math worksheet.

I pulled my list from my backpack and set it on my desk. Maybe if I stared at it long enough I'd be inspired.

Stare. Stare. Stare.

Nothing. Nothing. Nothing.

Fine, I'd do the math sheet first.

It was easy peasy lemon squeezy. So I was back to list-staring. Characters. Setting. Plot.

It was fine the way it was. Mrs. Finkel didn't know anything about writing books. I bet she hadn't written three by the time she was eight years old. Maybe she hasn't even written three books now, and she's . . . well, I don't know how old she is. That's not something teachers tell you.

But she's definitely way older than eight!

Still, there was no check mark on top of my paper.

"Dave!" Mom called, which is Dad's name—short for David. "Girls! Dinner!"

We all sat down at the table. I ate my rice. The salmon wasn't so bad if you mushed it up in rice.

"Just so you know, there's a surprise treat tonight," Dad told Penny.

"Is it more magic gum?" she asked. That was the last surprise treat Dad brought home. Penny loved it. But me, well, not so much. It ended up in my hair, and I had to get a VERY drastic haircut.

"Nope, not this time," Dad said.

That meant it was probably something better. But Penny seemed disappointed. "Can I have some anyway? I have a wish to make."

"What's that?"

"I wish Bruce would leave Somers and go back to his old school," Penny said.

For someone who didn't want to talk about him, she sure did mention him a lot.

"Maybe Bruce isn't so bad," Dad said. "Maybe he just got off on the wrong foot."

It was PENNY who used her foot, but still.

Mom leaned over and tapped her fork on the edge of my plate. "There seem to be a lot of asparagus spears left here," she said.

Ugh, the asparagus. You can't just mush it in rice to make it less gross. It's gross no matter what you do. In fact, it should be called asparaGROSS. So gross I had to pinch my nose closed to eat it.

(Here's some advice, if you have to eat something gross: pinch your nose so you won't taste the food as much. Because your taste buds and your nose are matched up inside your head. Or something like that.)

I ate the first spear of asparagross with my nose plugged up.

"Remember Stel, you promised to eat it or no treat," Mom said.

"Yeah," I said. "But I didn't promise to like it."

"I wish I could give Bruce all my asparagus," Penny said.

"You love vegetables, Penny," Mom reminded her.

"I know," Penny said. "But at lunch today, Bruce kept trying to trade his celery for something else, so I think maybe he doesn't like green things."

"Or maybe he just wasn't in the mood for

celery," Mom said.

"Nobody wanted to trade him though, because celery isn't anything like cookies or cupcakes. He said at his old school, people always traded him for celery."

"It's hard to be the new kid," Dad said. "Trust me, I know."

Dad moved around a lot when he was little. I always forget that except when he brings it up. In fact, I always forget that Dad was ever a little kid at all.

"Put yourself in Bruce's shoes," Dad said. "Imagine how he felt."

"But no one was in MY shoes. He said I didn't know the trading rules since I'm just a baby. I said that's not true. Then he said it's not true that Mom's having a baby, because I'm already a baby. And Miss Griffin called me up to her desk."

Penny wasn't the only Batts sister who got called up to her teacher's desk today, but I didn't say anything about that.

"It wasn't fair," Penny added.

"I think you're leaving out a little detail there, Pen," Mom said. I knew what detail she meant: the foot stomping.

"But *Bruce* started it, and then I had to go to Mr. O'Neil," Penny said. She started crying right then, which made her more upset, because crying is kind of a baby thing to do.

"But doesn't it make you feel a little bit better, now that you've told us your side of the story?" Dad asked.

Penny hiccupped and nodded. "A little," she said. "But I still don't like the ending of the story—that I got in trouble and Bruce didn't."

I had an idea right then. A really good one.

I pushed my seat back from the table and

stood up.

"Um, Stel," Mom said. "Aren't you forgetting something?"

"May I be excused?" I asked.

"You still have three asparagus spears left on your plate," Mom said.

I looked down. There they were. Well, fine,

they're not THAT gross. Not when they're the only thing in the way of getting to write down a really great idea. I picked them up and ate them so fast, it was probably breaking some kind of asparagus-eating world record.

"May I be excused *now*?" I asked.

"Yes," Mom said, at the same time that Dad said, "But you didn't have your treat."

"I'll have it later," I told him. "Right now I have homework to do."

CHAPTER 5

What Happens When You Try to Kill 'Em with Kindness

You probably want to hear all about my really good idea. But I'm too mad to write about it.

It's not because Mrs. Finkel thought it was a bad idea. She doesn't even know it yet.

It's something even worse.

Tuesday started off just regular. First Geography, then English. Then it was snack time, and that was when all the bad stuff happened.

Guess whose fault it was.

If you said Joshua, then you are EXACTLY RIGHT!!!

Here's what happened.

Mrs. Finkel said, "Okay, boys and girls, it's snack time. And if anyone has further questions about their short stories, feel free to come up and ask me. Anyone? Stella, do you want to talk about your progress?"

"No, I'm good," I said quickly. I hate when teachers single you out like that, and my cheeks got hot again. The really bad thing about blushing is that everyone can see how embarrassed you are.

I had Dad's surprise treat from the night before as my snack, so I ducked my head down and pulled it out from under my desk. It looked SO DELICIOUS. It was wrapped up in a clear plastic bag, tied with a red ribbon, like a present.

Usually I get up and stretch for the first half of snack time. Then Mrs. Finkel claps her hands and everyone returns to their own desks. That's when I eat. But this time, I thought maybe I'd just stay at my desk the whole time. The treat looked too good to wait any longer.

I untied the ribbon and started to pull off the plastic wrap, and then—

"Is that an ice-cream pop?" a voice asked. Joshua's voice. I looked up and there he was, standing next to my desk.

It did look sort of like an ice-cream pop, since it was on a stick and it had chocolate coating. "No," I said. Not that I knew for sure what it was. But it couldn't be ice cream, because that's too melty to take to school. "What is it then?"

"It's a secret," I told him.

"Secrets don't make friends," Joshua said. Like he would know anything about making friends. He didn't have any!

But then I remembered what Mr. King had said about Joshua being lonely. He didn't have friends, which made him mean, which made it so he didn't have friends. If I didn't tell him, did that make *me* a meanie?

So I said it, right then: "It's not really a secret. It's a surprise."

"Can I have it?" he asked.

"No," I said. I didn't say *no* in a mean way. It was my only snack, and he had his own snack at his desk. I was sure of it. "I'm supposed to taste-test it."

"How about just half?" he said. "I'll taste-test it with you."

Sometimes Penny and I are Official Batts

Confections Taste-Testers, but no one else is. And give him half? The treat was bigger than my usual snack, but still not that big.

Kill 'em with kindness, Mr. King had said.

Giving Joshua half would be a really REALLY kind thing.

It was the kind of thing Willa would have done, before she moved away to Pennsylvania. Like when Clark dropped the cupcake Arielle brought for her birthday, Willa shared hers with him. She was probably being nice and

sharing things with the kids in her new school right now. "Okay," I said. I pulled the wrapping off and broke it in half. One part stayed on the popsicle stick, and the other part didn't. I held that part out to Joshua.

"No fair!" he said. "You kept the bigger half!"

"It's my snack," I reminded him.

"Yeah, but my mom says one person gets to cut and the other gets to pick. That's the sharing rule."

"Hey Stella, aren't you coming over here?" Evie called to me.

Down the row, Lucy, Arielle, and Talisa were standing by Evie. Joshua swiped the bigger half of the treat off my desk. I put the other half down. I wasn't even excited about eating it anymore. "Coming," I said.

Joshua followed me over. I watched him

take a bite of his half—which really should have been MY half.

"Hey Joshua," Talisa said. "Knock, knock."

"Who's there?" he asked. But his mouth was full, so it sounded more like "Mooomp mooomp."

"Will," Talisa said.

"Will who?"

"Will you share that chocolate treat?"

Joshua shoved the rest of the pop in his mouth, and shook his head back and forth so hard that the sides of his hair lifted up a little bit. His hair is pretty short, so it didn't lift up too much. My hair is pretty short too, but not *that* short.

"I don't have any left," he said after he'd swallowed. "I only had half to begin with— Smella gave it to me."

There he was using that awful nickname

again. I guess I hadn't turned him nice yet.

"Do you have any for us too?" Lucy asked.

"No, sorry," I said. "I don't even know what it is yet."

"It tastes like fudge," Joshua said.

Oh, fudge on a stick! What a great brainchild! Fudge is one of my favorite things.

"You're not supposed to share with anyone if you can't share with the whole class," Lucy

told me. "That's one of Mrs. Finkel's rules."

Mrs. Finkel's rules are posted on the wall next to the coat closet. I knew about them, but I kind of forgot about that one when I gave Joshua half. And the only reason I did it was to NOT be a meanie.

Now I was a rule breaker—but so was Joshua. We're not supposed to eat our snacks when we're not at our desk, so he totally broke THAT rule.

"She has half left," Joshua said.

Wait a second!!! Joshua thought I should give up MY half! As Penny would say, that's not fair. And besides, it wasn't even big enough to split with everyone. "Joshua took the bigger half," I said.

"I had to test it because I'm going to have them at my party," Joshua explained. "My mom says we can have anything we want. As long as they sell it at Batts Confections, then we can have it."

"So then you'll get to have one," Evie told Lucy. "If you go to the party."

"I'm going," Lucy said.

I was about to say that I was going, too. But wait, we shouldn't have been talking about Joshua's party out in the open like that. What if Arielle wasn't invited? What if Talisa wasn't, or someone else who heard us talking? Then they would just feel bad. Like Clark, who sits on the other side of Evie. He could definitely hear us. If he heard us talking and he wasn't invited, he'd get hurt feelings.

"We shouldn't talk about it here," I said.

"Don't worry," Joshua said. "I invited the whole class except for one person, and she already knows about the party so it's okay."

Was it Talisa? Was it Arielle?

"Who?" Lucy asked.

"Smella!" Joshua said. "DUH!!!"

CHAPTER 6

Stamp of Approval

You can't just not invite someone to a party at their own store. That's a Ground Rule.

Okay not an official ground rule, like No Disruptive Behavior. But it should be one.

Penny had a play date after school—a makeup play date with Zoey because of what happened on Monday—but I didn't. My dad was the carpool driver. He said Mom was resting at home. After he dropped off Penny and Zoey, we headed to the store because he still had a bit of work to do.

"Can you do me a favor?" I asked.

"Certainly, darling," Dad said.

As soon as Dad said those words, "Certainly, darling," I felt better. Everything was going to be just fine—Dad would make sure of it.

"I need you to cancel Joshua's party at the store," I told him.

"But didn't you and Evie have plans to go to that together?"

"We did," I said. "But I didn't get to be invited. He invited everyone in my whole entire class except me!"

"I'm sure he didn't invite *everyone* else," Dad said.

"No, really," I insisted. "EVERYONE. That's what he said."

"Oh, darling, I'm so sorry," Dad said.

"That's why you have to cancel," I continued. "Leaving me out isn't allowed."

"I'm afraid it doesn't work that way, Stel," Dad said.

"Why not? It's OUR store."

"That's true, but I promised Joshua's mom we'd host the party."

"You made a promise to me too," I reminded him. "You said 'certainly' when I asked for a favor."

"Let me get this straight," Dad said. "This is Joshua, the boy in your class that you don't really like?"

"Yes," I said. "And I'm not the only one who doesn't like him. He's the biggest meanie I've ever known."

"If that's the case, then why do you *want* to go to the party?"

I didn't answer. The truth was, I didn't

really want to go. I just wanted to be invited.
I didn't say anything for a couple of minutes.
We stopped at a red light and Dad clicked the
rearview mirror down so he could see me in
the back seat. "What did you think about the
fudge pop?" he asked.

That's one of his Dad tricks—trying to
change the subject whenever Penny and I are
upset about something, so we stop thinking
about it. It works on Penny, but I'm older so
he can't distract me that easily.

"It was okay," I said glumly, still thinking
about Joshua.

"Just okay?"

I shrugged, but Dad didn't get to see my
shrug because the light turned green and his
eyes were back on the road.

"Maybe today you can help Stuart make
it great," he said.

When we got to the store, Dad and I took the elevator down to level C, which means cellar—another word for basement. He had a few things to do in his office. I sat at the desk, watching him sort through papers.

"Where are last week's receipts? Oh here they are," Dad said. I knew he wasn't talking to me. He talks to himself when he's thinking about work stuff. "I think the new samples are upstairs. I'm going to head up."

I spun around on his desk chair.

"I think the new samples are upstairs. I'm going to head up," Dad repeated.

Oh, he was talking to me this time. I stopped spinning.

"How long will you be gone?"

"Not long," he said. "Do you have homework to do?"

I shook my head, no. The only homework

for the night was working on our short stories, and mine was nearly done—sitting on my desk at home.

"I'll just be a few minutes," Dad said. "Then we can go home." He started to walk out the door, but then turned and came back

toward me. He reached over my head for a stack of papers. "I know what you can do," he said, handing me the pile. "You can put these order forms in alphabetical order by last name—here, see the last names on the tops of the page?"

I nodded. "What are they orders for?"

"Gift baskets, party supplies, that sort of thing. Can you do it? It would actually help me out a lot."

"Sure," I said.

I got started as soon as he left. It wasn't a hard job. Even Penny could do it. After all, kindergarteners know the letters in the alphabet. Kids even younger than kindergarten know that.

I tucked "WASSERMAN, Robert" behind "MILLER, Dawn" because "W" comes after "M" in the alphabet, and flipped to the next form.

And there it was: "LEWIS, Joshua." The order form for Joshua's party.

He'd ordered marzipan cookie sculpture-making kits—enough for twenty-one kids.

My stomach felt strange suddenly, like it

was turning somersaults inside my body.

What would Joshua do if he was the one—the ONLY one—not invited to a party?

First thing, I bet he'd slam his hand down on the desk. Whack! Loud! Disruptive Behavior!

Then he'd probably tear up the order form.

He'd tear it in half, and in half again.

He'd keep on tearing until it was just eensy weensy pieces of paper and you wouldn't even be able to tell it was ever an order form. He'd throw the pieces up in the air like confetti, and not even care that he'd ruined everything.

Wow, that's a really mean thing to do, I thought. I'd never do anything like that. Even though, well, I sort of really wanted to.

I didn't even want to think about Joshua right then, so I put his form down on Dad's

desk for now and moved on. NICHOLS, Faye. KEANE, Mary. The last form was ZELNICK, Jordan.

The door opened. I swiveled around in my chair.

"Stella Batts!" Stuart said. "I heard you were in here. I'm wondering if I can enlist your help—that is, if you're not too busy."

I shook my head. "I just finished putting the order forms in alphabetical order," I told him.

"Great," he said. "Then come with me."

I stood up and put the pile of forms on top of Dad's file cabinet. Stuart and I went into the kitchen, which is the room right next to the office. Most of the candy we sell at the store comes ready-made, so we don't need a big kitchen. But we do make cookies and fudge ourselves. Stuart had batches of fresh fudge on the counter.

I can't tell you our fudge recipe, because that's a family secret. Okay, not exactly a family secret, since Stuart knows it and he's not in our family. But it's still something I'm not supposed to tell.

"I'm working on some new fudge flavors,"

Stuart told me. "I thought you'd want to taste."

The recipes might be a secret, but I can tell you the new flavors—s'mores, red velvet, white chocolate, cookies and cream, and banana split. Stuart gave me eensy weensy slivers of each—except for the banana-split one, because I don't really like fruit to be in my dessert.

"So?" he asked.

"Good," I said. "Really, really good."

"The Stella Batts stamp of approval for Stella's Fudge," Stuart said. "Now I'm ready to go."

"Are you going to turn these into your new brainchild?" I asked.

"You mean fudge pops? I don't see why not," he said.

I helped him cut the pans of fudge up into smaller squares. Then we stuck sticks in

them. Stuart heated up the chocolate sauce for dipping. "I think they need a little something more, don't you?" Stuart asked. "They taste delicious, but I don't know if they look special enough."

"I'll think about it," I said.

We kept on dipping the pops. I didn't even notice that Dad had come in until he started speaking. "How's it going in here?"

"Good," Stuart and I both said. Stuart's practically a grownup, so I didn't say jinx—even though that's what you're supposed to say if someone says the exact same thing at the exact same time.

"How's Elaine feeling?" Stuart asked Dad. Elaine is my mom.

"She's happy this baby is coming soon," Dad said. "If all goes according to schedule, Stella and Penny will have a little brother next week."

"If you need anything, just let me know," Stuart said.

"Thanks," Dad said. "My mother-in-law is coming this weekend, so we'll have a lot of help at home. But could you take care of the order forms Stella just alphabetized? They're on my desk."

"On the file cabinet," I corrected.

We said goodbye to Stuart and headed home.

CHAPTER 7

Don't Scratch Your Nose

For the next two days, Mom and Dad were super busy getting ready for the baby. I was busy too, finishing up my story.

Thursday night, it was all finished. I read it over again, and again one more time, just to make sure all the story ingredients were really in there. They were:

Characters, check!

Setting, check!

Plot, check!

I copied the whole thing down on another piece of paper, in my absolute best handwriting.

I put the story into a folder (so it wouldn't get crinkled) and into my backpack. Then I clicked my heels together and whispered a little wish that Mrs. Finkel really would love it.

"What was that?" Mom asked, walking into my room.

"Just my story," I told her.

"What story?"

"The homework Mrs. Finkel gave us for the week," I said.

"That's perfect homework for you!"

"Yeah," I agreed. "Except Mrs. Finkel also said she didn't think I knew how to write a story."

"She really said that?"

"Sort of. We handed in descriptions

of our characters, setting, and plot, and she didn't like mine."

"Can I read the story now?" Mom asked. "You're not too busy?"

"Oh, Stel," Mom said. "I know I've been distracted with all things baby these days. But I'm still your mom and I'll always have time to read your stories."

I pulled the folder out of my backpack and handed it over.

"It's about platypuses?" Mom asked.

"Just one," I said. "A platypus named Penelope, but she's in school with all different kinds of animals. You should go into the other room to read it because real writers don't get to watch when other people read their books."

"You got it," Mom said. She walked out and came back in a few minutes later.

"What did you think?"

"It was very poignant," she said. "Do you know what that means?"

"Yeah," I said. "Not really."

"It means moving, heartfelt," she said. "You know the part where the goose came in and told Penelope the platypus she wasn't allowed to go into the water anymore?"

"Yeah?"

"I really felt her frustration. And the part

where the poison came out of her foot—"

"That's a real thing!" I said. "Platypuses shoot poison from their feet when creatures are mean to them. I read it in one of Penny's platypus books. That's why Penelope the platypus didn't get in trouble—she couldn't help herself!"

"I think the real Penny will like that part of the story."

"I wrote it for her," I said.

"I figured," Mom said. "You know what might make this story feel complete? If the goose and the platypus can come to some sort of truce at the end?"

"So you don't think it's good, either?"

"Of course I think it's good. I think it's great, actually. It's just that there's always room for improvement. Maybe that's what Mrs. Finkel was trying to tell you."

"Do you think she'll like my story if I improve it?"

"I hope so," Mom said. "But that's the thing about stories. Readers have different tastes and they don't always agree on what's great. Do you understand what I'm saying?"

I nodded. Sometimes people wouldn't like my stories. It made me feel like crying, just a little bit, like when you eat jalapeño jelly beans and your eyes get watery. "I don't like this week," I said.

"I'm sorry," Mom told me. "The good thing is that it's almost over. Just one more day to get through."

"Except tomorrow is Friday—Joshua's birthday party day, and that'll be the worst day of all."

"Try not to think about it too much," she said.

"I am trying not to think about it," I told her. "I just can't help myself."

"You're right," Mom said. "That was a silly thing to tell you. When you're trying not to think about something, that's when you think about it the most. Like what would happen if I told you not to scratch your nose? Whatever you do, don't scratch it. It doesn't itch."

"Wait, it *does* itch right now! But it didn't until you just said that. Now my nose is itchy and I'm still thinking about Joshua," I told her.

"*I'm* thinking about your story," Mom said. "I happen to think it's one of your best. Are you going to tell Penny about it?"

I shook my head. "Not until I know for sure that Mrs. Finkel likes it. Then I'll tell

Penny."

"I heard my name," Penny said, bounding into the room. "That means you were talking about me."

"I was just saying how much I love my girls," Mom said. She winked at me. "And how that won't change when the baby comes."

Penny cuddled up to Mom on the bed. "You know what I was thinking about the baby?" Penny asked. "We don't know what it looks like yet. Isn't that funny?"

"That's the thing about having a baby," Mom said. "You never know what you're going to get. But I think Dad and I did all right the first couple of times around, so I'm not particularly worried."

Penny yawned, which made me yawn. "I think that's the signal that it's time to get ready for bed," Mom said.

"I still have time before bed, right?" I asked. I'm three years older, so I always get to stay up later than Penny.

"A little bit of time," Mom said.

After she and Penny headed out, I reread my story again. Mom was right. There was something missing from the end. But I fixed it. Then I went to sleep.

CHAPTER 8

All My Fault

And then I woke up. It was Friday. The day of Joshua's birthday party.

Mrs. Benson was driving to school. She pulled up outside our house. Mom walked us to the front door. "Have a good day, girls," she said.

But I knew having a good day would be impossible.

"I'll be here when you get home," she said.

"Can Evie come over?" I asked.

"Evie's going to Joshua's party," she reminded me.

"Actually I don't think she'll want to go without me," I said. "She's new, after all."

"I'm sorry, Stel," Mom said. "Mrs. King called me last night. She said Daddy doesn't have to pick Evie up from school today, because Evie is going home with Lucy. They're going to head over to Joshua's party together."

"Does that mean you'll play with me after school?" Penny asked hopefully. "Zoey has to go to the dentist, so it'll just be you and me. Hooray!"

"You see," Mom said, bending to kiss the top of my head. "Someone thinks you're very special."

It was just Penny who thought so, but I didn't point that out.

"Go on now," Mom told us. "The Bensons

are waiting."

When we got to school, Mrs. Finkel collected our stories first thing. "I'm very excited to read all these," she said. "It will be like reading an anthology. Does anyone know what 'anthology' means?"

Anthology is the kind of big word that I like, and I did know what it meant. There's a section at the new bookstore, Scheherazade, labeled "ANTHOLOGIES" and I asked Dad about it. He told me an anthology is a group of stories that are connected in some way, like they could be all about the same thing.

But I didn't raise my hand. I just let Mrs. Finkel explain. She said our stories were connected because we're all in the same class, even though the subjects were all different.

Then Joshua waved his hand around. Mrs. Finkel called on him. "But there are

two dragon stories, so not everything is different. Maybe Asher should've written about something else."

"Now, Joshua," Mrs. Finkel said. "I've had enough of that. The stories will be different because they have different authors—or you could have picked another subject to write about. You don't want to go to Mr. O'Neil today, on your actual birthday, do you?"

"That would be against the rules," Joshua told her.

Mrs. Finkel MAKES the Ground Rules—I think she knows what's for or against them. "We can certainly have two stories about dragons," is all she said.

See how mean Joshua is to Asher! But he still invited Asher to his party, and Asher was probably going.

I wish I would stop thinking about Joshua's stupid party, I thought to myself. I clicked my heels three times under my desk.

It didn't work.

Kids were talking about the party at snack time and again at lunch. Everyone was going, except for Clark and Maddie, and not because they didn't want to. Clark had to go visit his great-aunt, and Maddie has jazz dance on Fridays.

"It's too bad that you have to miss a party at Batts Confections," Lucy told her.

All the other kids nodded in agreement.

That's the problem with having the coolest store in all of Somers, California—everyone wants to go to parties there.

Actually, it's never been a problem before. It was just a problem TODAY.

Finally school was over. Even if I didn't get to go to the party, at least I got to go home.

I headed out to the flagpole, but Dad wasn't the one standing with Penny. It was Stuart! What was Stuart doing at Somers Elementary School? He's in college!

"Hiya Stella, I have some exciting news," he started.

But he didn't get to finish what he was saying, because Penny jumped in. "Mom's having the baby!" she yelled. "Right now!"

"That's right," Stuart said.

"But the baby isn't supposed to be here until next week," I said. "Grandma doesn't get here until this weekend."

"I guess the baby wasn't aware of the schedule," Stuart said. "So you girls are stuck with me."

I didn't mind being stuck with Stuart. He's got a cool car. It's blue, which is my new favorite color, and there are only two doors instead of four. To get into the back seat, Stuart had to pull a lever to make the front seat fold over. Then we climbed in and he pushed the front seat back up.

"I'll tell you the way to get home," Penny said. I bet Stuart already knew, but he pretended like he needed Penny's help with the directions. When we got to the house, she told him the rules, like how we have to take our shoes off when we get inside, and how we get a snack.

"What kind of snack?" Stuart asked.

"Sometimes apples or grapes or cheese and crackers," I said.

"Or candy," Penny said. "As much as we want!"

That part wasn't really true, but I didn't correct her.

We went to the kitchen. Stuart gave us each a Batts chocolate bar and a glass of milk. He washed off some strawberries, put them in a bowl, and placed them in the middle of the table. We all sat down. "There," he said.

"If you take a bite of strawberry and a bite of the bar, it'll be like eating chocolate-covered strawberries."

"Oh yum!" Penny said. She turned to Stuart. "Stella and I are having a sisters' play date today, but you can play too. I made a list of things we should do."

"I always make lists," I said.

"I know," Penny said. "That's how I got the idea to make one. Hold on—I'll get it." She ran out to the front hall and came back with her backpack. "Here it is," she said, pulling out a crinkled piece of paper.

Penny doesn't know how to spell so well yet. Some of the words didn't even have vowels. But she read it to me:

1. Stella will teach me how to play Spit
2. We can pretend to be twins
3. Stella will write a book and she will let me do the pictures

Just then some music started playing from inside Stuart's pocket. He pulled out his cell phone. "That must be someone calling from the store," he said.

"How do you know?" I asked.

"I programmed my phone to play the Candy Man song." He pressed the "talk" button. "Hello?" he said.

Muffled sounds came from Stuart's cell phone. I couldn't make out the voice or the words, but it sounded like someone was upset.

"Calm down," he said. "Tell me exactly what happened."

There were more muffled words.

Then Stuart said, "No, we can't bother Dave about this." Dave is my dad, in case you don't remember. "I never saw a form for Lewis."

Uh-oh, that meant an order form was probably missing.

Wait! Did he say Lewis? That was Joshua's last name! Oh no!!!

I *did* see an order form for Joshua Lewis. I left it on Dad's desk, not on the file cabinet with all the other order forms.

"I'll be there as soon as possible," Stuart said. He hung up the phone, pushed his chair back and stood up. "Girls, there's a party problem at the store."

"Parties aren't problems," Penny said.

"They are when no one knows they're happening. We're missing an order form—so we have a lot of kids showing up, and a birthday boy, and no party. They need my help over there so we have to head to the store."

"But I can't go," I said. "I wasn't invited."

"You don't need to be invited," Stuart said. "The store has your name on it."

I shook my head.

"I wasn't invited either," Penny sniffed.

"We can stay here and I'll watch Penny," I offered.

"And I can watch Stella," Penny added.

Stuart shook his head. "I made a promise to your parents that I'd take care of you two. I can't leave you alone."

The truth was, I would've been scared to stay home with just Penny anyway. But I was scared of the store too.

"Come on," Stuart said. "I need to leave now to get this sorted out."

Now I had to go to Joshua's party. And it was all my fault.

CHAPTER 9

Stella Superhero (Again)

My heart was pounding in my chest like THUMP THUMP THUMP.

It was worse than the time when the mean lunch aide Mr. Moyers took my writing notebook away.

Worse than when the magic gum got caught in my hair.

Worse than when I had to climb through a tiny window in the back of Evie's dad's truck and rescue the keys.

Worse than when I was worried Willa wouldn't want to talk to me again.

Okay, actually maybe not worse than that last one. But it was at least a tie, because this time there were two things to worry about:

1. I had to go to a party that I wasn't invited to

AND

2. The reason I had to go was because I'd lost the order form.

I didn't do it on purpose, but I still felt like such a meanie.

As soon as we walked into the store, Claire and Jess rushed over to us. They're two other workers at Batts Confections.

"Stuart!" Jess called. "Oh, Stuart! Thank goodness you're here. We had no idea this was happening, until twenty-five kids showed up!"

"Where is everyone?" Stuart asked.

"In the party room. We placed an order for pizza, but we don't have an activity to entertain them."

"How about cookie decorating?" Stuart suggested. I made a batch of cookies last night."

"I suggested that," Claire said. "The birthday boy said he did that already on a class trip."

That's right, he did. The last time my whole entire class was at the store. But that time, I was invited too.

"His mother is not happy," Jess added.

"It's all right," Stuart said. "I'll go talk to the mother and try to smooth things over. We'll figure something out. Stella, Penny, why don't you girls come with me? It may help to have some real Batts family representatives with me."

Go with Stuart? Into the party room where Joshua was? I knew exactly what he would say when he saw me: *Smella, what are you doing here? I didn't invite YOU.*

What if he could tell by looking at me that the whole thing was my fault?

There was no way I was going upstairs to that party room. But I didn't want to stay where I was, either. If someone from Mrs. Finkel's class came down to use the bathroom, they'd know I was the girl who wasn't invited, and I was only there because there was a mess-up at the store.

"Ready?" Stuart asked.

I shook my head. "I'm going to go to my dad's office, if that's all right," I said.

"Oh no, I'm not going down there," Penny said. "That's where they put the giant clown."

There's supposed to be
a clown mannequin in the
candy circus display when
you walk into the store. But
Penny was really scared of
it, so Stuart moved it down
to the basement. Now
the clown is leaning up
against the back corner
in Dad's office. I barely
even noticed it. That's how not scared of it I
was.

"You don't have to come with me," I said.
"I'll go by myself—I'm allowed to." I added
that last part so Stuart would know that letting
me go to the office on my own was not the
same as leaving me home on my own.

"And I'll go upstairs with you," Penny
told Stuart.

She reached for his hand. She gets scared just *thinking* about the clown.

"All right," Stuart said. "But Stel, don't wander anywhere else, okay?"

"Okay," I said.

I took the elevator down to level C, headed into Dad's office and closed the door. I didn't want to look at his desk too closely, in case the order form was there, smack in the middle.

Except I couldn't help looking. There were framed photos of our family, Dad's big calendar, a couple of folders, and a bunch of loose papers. But there was nothing that looked like an order form.

Where could it be?

Did I just imagine that it was here once?

If I made the whole thing up, then it wasn't really my fault.

I sat down in the swirly chair. My heart was still thump-thumping, like Pop Rocks were exploding inside of me. Suddenly Penny burst into the room.

"He's up there," she cried. "In the party room!"

"I know," I said miserably. "It's his party."

Penny knows just how mean Joshua can be. When I got my hair cut short, he said I didn't look like a girl anymore. Penny tried to take his candy away from him, but Mom wouldn't let her.

"Ah!" Penny cried some more. "But the clown is here! He's even worse than before! Help me, Stella!"

She backed up against the door. Her eyes were super wide, so I knew she was really REALLY scared.

"Penny, it's okay," I told her. "It's just pretend." I stood up from the swirly chair. "I can show you he's not so scary."

I started to walk toward the clown, but the closer I got, the scarier it looked. I didn't want to get too near to it. Penny had her eyes shut tight anyway.

"You have to come with me," she said. "I can't go upstairs alone."

"Did Joshua say something to you?" I asked. "Did he call you a mean name?"

What mean thing rhymes with Penny? I couldn't think of a thing. But I'll tell you what I *was* thinking—I was done trying to kill him with kindness. If he hurt Penny's feelings then I was glad I'd ruined his birthday. He deserved it!

Penny shook her head. She cracked open her eyes so they were little dark slits, like thin strips of licorice. "No, not Joshua," she said. "Bruce!"

Bruce? What was he doing at Batts Confections?

Penny and I went up to the first floor. "Let's wait for Stuart here," I said, pulling Penny toward the register. It was the perfect place, because you can sit to the side of it, and then no one can see you.

But Penny tugged on my hand. "We have to go to the party room," she said.

"I thought you didn't want to see Bruce."

"I don't want to see him by myself," she corrected. "I want to see him with you."

"But why? I don't even know Bruce."

"You know *me*," Penny said. "And you can tell him that I'm not a baby. He'll believe you because you're in third grade."

Penny thinks I'm really big. I forget that

sometimes.

Upstairs, everyone in my whole entire class was seated around the table. Except not Maddie and not Clark because they couldn't come. And obviously not me, because I wasn't invited.

And not Joshua either. He and his mom were across the room. They didn't see us come in. *Please DON'T turn around*, I thought to myself. *Please don't see me.* If I had a piece of magic gum right then, I'd wish for Joshua to NEVER see me.

But I wanted other people to keep on seeing me. Like Evie. She was sitting at the far end of the table, in between Lucy and Talisa. She looked up and smiled, so I could tell she was happy I was there after all. "Hey Stella!" she called out.

Penny was hanging on my side as I

walked over toward them, which made me walk a bit slower than usual.

"Do you have cards?" Lucy asked me.

"Cards? You mean a birthday card?"

There was no way I was going to give Joshua a card if he didn't invite me to his party!

"No," Lucy said. "Cards to play with. We don't have an activity yet, so I thought we could play Spit."

I shook my head. "Sorry."

"Joshua doesn't want to do any of the activities the people keep suggesting," Talisa explained.

"It's getting boring," Lucy added.

"Oh look, the baby is here," a boy said.

I knew it was the boy named Bruce even before Penny whispered, "That's him, that's him."

"What are you doing here, baby?"

Penny squeezed up even tighter to me, sticking to me like she was a piece of caramel. "It's my store," she told him. But she said it so soft and mumbly, the way she speaks when she's scared of something. I didn't think he could hear her.

But I wasn't scared of Bruce. "It's our store," I said, loudly.

"No it's not."

"Yes it is," Lucy told him.

"It's called Batts Confections," I said. "That's us. The Batts sisters. Did you see the candy circus downstairs?" I asked. "Penny helped set it up. A baby can't do that. Actually most five-year-olds wouldn't have even been able to set it up. But Penny is very mature for her age."

"Who are *you*?" Bruce asked.

"Stella Batts," I said.

"You're Penny's sister?"

"Yup," I said. "Her older sister. Who are you?"

"I'm Joshua's cousin," Bruce said.

They were cousins?! Mrs. Finkel was right! Sometimes the writer knows the end of the story before it even happens.

"Hey Joshua," Talisa called. "Did you decide on an activity yet?"

I turned around and there he was, looking right back at me. He came right over and I squeezed myself up tighter to Penny, like I was the little sister, right then.

"No," he told Talisa. "This is my worst birthday ever. I wish I'd never even heard of Batts Confections. I'm never setting foot in this place again."

It was a mean thing to say, but I felt an eensy weensy bit glad. It was okay with me if he never set foot in the store again!

"I told you that you had to share that pop with me," he said.

"What does the pop have to do with it?" I asked.

"You owed me something for my birthday," he said.

That didn't make any sense. But suddenly I had an idea.

"Hey Stuart," I called.

Stuart was talking to Mrs. Lewis and he didn't hear me right away. "Stuart," I said again.

"One minute, Stel," he said. "Mrs. Lewis and I are trying to settle on a party activity."

"This is about the activity," I told him.

"Well, come over here then," he said. I did. Penny followed me and Bruce followed her and Joshua followed all three of us.

"I have an idea. But first I need to know if we have a good amount of fudge—enough for everyone."

"We do," Stuart said.

"But there's a problem," Bruce said. "I don't like chocolate and that's what fudge is made of."

"That's crazy," Penny said. "Everyone likes fudge."

"Especially our fudge," Stuart said. "But don't worry, we have plenty of flavors—vanilla, strawberry, maple syrup, to name a few."

"Great," I said. "And fudge is smushable, like clay or marzipan. So how about if all the kids make fudge sculptures. They can put them on a stick to make lollipops and dip them in chocolate."

"Ew, chocolate," Bruce said.

"Or caramel," I said. "If you like that better. And decorate them with sprinkles and stuff. That would make the pops look special, right Stuart?"

"Joshua?" Mrs. Lewis asked.

"YES!!!!" Joshua said.

"All right, Stella," Stuart said. "You saved the day. You must have some sort of candy connection, to think of something so clever."

Obviously Stuart was kidding because he already KNOWS my candy connection.

He got the ingredients and I helped him, Jess, and Claire set everything up.

"You can sit near me," Bruce called to Penny.

"I want to stay with my sister," Penny said.

"We'll squeeze and make room for you guys," Evie said, scooting over a bit.

"There's not really enough room," I said.

"Of course there's room for you, Stella," Mrs. Lewis said from behind me. "I'm so glad you came after all. We didn't get your response, so I thought maybe your mom was too busy planning for the new baby."

"I never got invited," I told her.

"What do you mean? We mailed you an invitation, just the same as everyone else. Joshua, did you know Stella didn't get the invite?"

Of course Joshua knew I didn't get the invite. He was the one who told me I wasn't invited. He must've hidden the invitation, or thrown it away, before his mother could mail it!

Across the table, Joshua suddenly had a look on his face like he knew he was about to get in trouble.

There was a part of me that felt glad about that.

But it was his birthday. And I was done being a meanie. "It was probably just the mail," I said. "You know even if you mail things at all the same time, sometimes they arrive at different times. I bet the invitation will be waiting for me when I get home."

"But you're staying now, right?" Lucy asked.

"You invented our activity," Mrs. Lewis said. "You should stay—your sister too."

"It's fine with me, if you want to," Stuart said.

I shook my head. "No thanks," I said. "We have to go home and wait for my mom to call. She's in the hospital right now having a baby."

"That's very exciting," Mrs. Lewis said.

"It is," I told her. Then I looked over at Joshua. "Happy birthday," I said to him.

CHAPTER 10

Chocolate Twenty-Dollar Bills

Stuart had a great idea to bring the ingredients home. We both decided to make fudge sculptures for the baby. Penny used milk-chocolate and white-chocolate swirled fudge, and I used cookies-and-cream fudge.

"Mmmm," Penny said, licking her fingers. "Can you believe Bruce doesn't like chocolate? I mean, it's crazy not to like chocolate. EVERYONE likes chocolate."

"Not everyone," Stuart said. "Unless

you're a twenty-dollar bill, not everyone is going to like you."

"But a person can't be a twenty-dollar bill," Penny said.

"That's exactly what I mean," Stuart said. "Most people in the world are going to love you, the same as most people in the world love chocolate. But you'll encounter a few people along the way who have different tastes. It may not make sense to you and me, but there isn't really anything you can do to change it."

"Like Joshua," I said. "He doesn't like me."

"And Bruce," Penny said. "He doesn't like me. Except now I think he sort of does, because he knows I have a candy store."

"Joshua knew that all along and it didn't make him like me," I said. "I tried to be extra nice but it didn't change his mind. He's still a meanie to me."

"Let me ask you something, Stella," Stuart said. "Do you think you're a likeable person?"

"Yeah," I said.

"I like you," Penny piped up. "I love you. You're the most favorite big sister I ever had."

"I'm the only big sister you've ever had."

"I know!" Penny said. "So that makes you my least favorite, too." She giggled to herself, enjoying her joke.

"Do you like you?" Stuart asked me. His voice was pretty serious.

I nodded.

"Why?" he asked.

"I think I'm a nice girl. I think I'm fun and smart."

"All right," he said. "That's the most

important thing. Be the kind of person that YOU think is a good, likeable person."

"Stories are like that, too," I said. "Not everyone is going to like the same stories."

"Exactly," Stuart said. "So you just do your best, and don't worry about everyone else. You should still be kind to Joshua, because that will make you feel good about yourself. What he thinks in return doesn't matter so much."

"That's why I was nice to him at the party," I said. "I wanted to make it up to him after I .. . after I lost the order form. I put it on the desk instead of the file cabinet with the others. The whole thing was my fault, you know."

"Ah, but it wasn't," Stuart said. "Your dad put it with the other forms. But then when your mom called and said it was time to go the hospital, he was in such a rush packing up things he needed from the store, he accidentally brought a few order forms with him. Joshua's just happened to be one of them."

"Really?" I asked.

"Really," Stuart said.

"I just thought of something!" Penny said. "What about a chocolate twenty-dollar bill? Would everyone like that?"

"Maybe so," Stuart said.

She held up her fudge sculpture. "I'm done!" she announced. "What do you think?"

I didn't want to hurt her feelings, but I couldn't tell what she'd made. "It looks like a J," I said.

"It is a J!" she said. "For baby Jack! He should be born by now, don't you think?"

"Mom and Dad would've called," I said.

"Maybe they'll call right now," Penny said. She turned toward the phone on the counter.

"Three, two, one, ring!"

The phone rang about twenty minutes later, after I'd finished making my own fudge sculptures—a rattle and a little duck.

Stuart answered. I heard him say, "That's wonderful, Elaine! Oh yes, they're right here. Hold on."

He handed Penny the receiver because she was closest. But she let me share it with her, both of our ears pressed against it. "Congratulations, girls," Mom said. "You're both big sisters! You have a little brother."

"Yippee!" Penny said.

"When can we meet him?" I asked.

"Daddy will bring you by in the morning. And when you see him tonight, he'll have lots of pictures. He's a cute little guy. He looks a

little bit like each of you."

I felt the eensy weensiest little tears in my eyes. Sometimes being really happy makes that happen.

"Stella, I'm sorry I wasn't there for you when you got home today," Mom said. "I know you were sad about everything with Joshua."

"Stuart had to go to the store so I saw the

party," I said.

"Oh honey."

"No, it's okay," I told her. "It actually wasn't so bad."

"I'm glad," Mom said. "I love you so much. I love both you girls so much."

"Us too," I said.

"And baby Jack too!" Penny said. "Tell him we love him!"

"Oh, I knew I was forgetting something!" Mom said. "His name isn't Jack. It's Marco. Marco Benjamin Batts. What do you think?"

"That's a great name," I told her.

Mom said she had to go, but that Daddy would be home before too long. We said goodbye.

When we hung up, I noticed Penny eyeing her J-shaped piece of fudge. "Don't be sad," I told her. "It's still smushable. You can just smush it into an M."

"I'm not sad," Penny said. "I was just thinking. Little babies can't eat fudge. I should eat it for him."

She picked up the J and took a big bite. "Yummers," she said. "This was a good day."

You know what? I had to agree.

"Hey, Penny," I said. "I have a story to show you."

Bonus
(That means extra stuff)

A STORY FOR MY SISTER
by Stella Batts

Once upon a time there was a duck-billed platypus named Penelope. In case you don't know how to say that name, it's Pa-nell-o-pee. (Not Peen-lope.)

Penelope went to school and had a bunch of friends. Plus, she had a platypus sister. Her sister was older so they weren't in the same class.

But there were lots of other kids in Penelope's class, all different kinds of animals. Penelope liked them all. That is, until Bruce the Goose started at her school.

Penelope had played with geese before. She thought it would be just fine. At recess that day, Penelope went to play in the pond. Bruce waddled over and honked to get Penelope's attention.

"You need to get out right now," he told her.

Oh no! Was there something wrong with the water? Was it a monster?

Penelope leaped out of the water as quick as she could. But then Bruce went right in!

"Be careful!" she called. "It's not safe."

"Of course it's safe," Bruce said.

"Then why did you make me get out?"

"Geese have first choice," he explained. "That's the rule. So I traded you—my spot on dry land for your water spot."

Geese did NOT have first choice. Penelope crawled toward the water to go in again. Bruce honked extra loud, which made her jump back as far as she could. (Which wasn't too far because she had stubby little duck-billed platypus legs, not so good for jumping.)

"This is not fair," Penelope said.

And then something happened. The same thing that always happened when Penelope thought something was not fair. A little bit of poison shot out of her foot. It wasn't killer poison, but it was the hurting kind. It landed splat on Bruce's left wing.

"Ow! Ow! Ow! Ow! Ow!" he cried.

The teacher, Miss Griffin, heard his crying and raced over.

"That horrible platypus stung me with her poison," he tattled. "You have to punish her."

But Penelope couldn't help herself. It was just what happened to duck-billed platypuses when they got upset. Which meant Bruce had to have been mean first.

The one who starts the trouble is the one who should get in trouble. That's the rule—the real rule.

"Come out of the water, Bruce," Miss Griffin said. "I'm sending you to the principal."

"Yeah, Bruce," Penny said. "You're going to the principal."

Bruce waddled out of the water. But then something happened to Penny. She started to feel bad. Even if it wasn't her fault, she'd still hurt him—on his first day at school. And now he was going to have to go to the principal on his first day. Plus, her big sister's class let out for recess right then. She wasn't even upset about not being in the water anymore.

"Wait, Miss Griffin," Penelope said. "You don't have to punish Bruce. He didn't know the rules for our school. And I think getting hurt with platypus poison is all the punishment he needs."

"If you're sure," Miss Griffin said.

Penelope nodded. She was sure. "I'm sorry I hurt you, Bruce," she added. "Want to come meet my sister?"

He honked again, but a softer honk this time. A honk that meant, "Okay."

So Penelope took Bruce over to meet the big kids. And here's something funny. He already knew the goose named Joshua in her sister's class. It was his cousin!

After that, Penelope taught Bruce a big-kid card game called Spit. She let Bruce win, since it was his first day, and she still felt a little bad about the hurting poison.

But next time, he'd have to win fair and square, because she'd play her best.

THE END

Courtney Sheinmel

Courtney Sheinmel is the author of several books for middle-grade readers, including *Sincerely* and *All The Things You Are*. Like Stella Batts, she was born in California and has a younger sister. However, her parents never owned a candy store. Now Courtney lives in New York City, where she has tasted all the cupcakes in her neighborhood. She also makes a delicious cookie brownie graham-cracker pie. Visit her at www.courtneysheinmel.com, where you can find the recipe along with information about all the Stella Batts books.

Jennifer A. Bell

Jennifer A. Bell is a children's book illustrator whose work can also be found in magazines, on greeting cards, and on the occasional Christmas ornament. She studied Fine Arts at the Columbus College of Art and Design and currently lives in Minneapolis, Minnesota.

In this early chapter book series, the ups and downs of Stella's life are charmingly chronicled. She's in third grade, she wants to be a writer, and her parents own a candy shop. Life should be sweet, right?

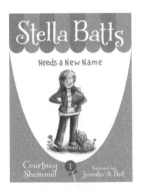

Praise for Stella Batts:

"Sheinmel has a great ear for the dialogue and concerns of eight-year-old girls. Bell's artwork is breezy and light, reflecting the overall tone of the book. This would be a good choice for fans of Barbara Park's 'Junie B. Jones' books."

— *School Library Journal*

"First in a series featuring eight-year-old Stella, Sheinmel's unassuming story, cheerily illustrated by Bell, is a reliable read for those first encountering chapter books. With a light touch, Sheinmel persuasively conveys elementary school dynamics; readers may recognize some of their own inflated reactions to small mortifications in likeable Stella, while descriptions of unique candy confections are mouth-watering."

— *Publisher's Weekly*

Other books in this series:

Stella Batts Needs a New Name
Stella Batts: Hair Today, Gone Tomorrow
Stella Batts: Pardon Me

Meet Stella and friends online at www.stellabatts.com